The Adventures of Petey the Chiweenie

Learning Acceptance

CARLA TUCKER MINKS

Illustrated by

Deborah Wyman

PERSONA PUBLISHING

Published by

Casa Grande, Arizona

The Adventures of Petey the Chiweenie: Learning Acceptance

Copyright ©2019 by Carla Tucker Minks

Edited by Marylou Mylant and Kathy Sewright

Story, design and composition by Carla Tucker Minks

The illustrations were rendered in pencil and ink by Deborah Wyman

ISBN 978-1-5136-5595-6

10 9 8 7 6 5 4 3 2 1

First Edition

This book is dedicated to all the dogs in shelters across the country.

My heart is full for those people who adopt from shelters in an effort to reduce the number of pets needlessly euthanized each year. I also want to thank Marylou Mylant and Kathy Sewright for their time reading and editing and encouraging me to finish this journey with Petey. Lastly, without Petey I wouldn't have the stories to tell and laughs to share.

— Carla

Petey's mama, Izzy, was a Dachshund, a very low-to-the-ground dog with super short legs. That means she wasn't made for running far or jumping in the air, but these short-legged hounds are game for just about anything else. She was smart and alert, with a big-dog bark, that made her a good watchdog.

Petey is a cute and active little dog. He looks a lot like a Chihuahua, but a little different. You see, Petey's dad was a Chihuahua – strong and mighty.

Petey's daddy, Freckle, was a spunky tan-colored Chihuahua with a big-dog attitude and weighed no more than 6 pounds. Chihuahuas are known for their round "apple" shaped head and ears that stand up very straight. They also have full, bright eyes. Petey got most of his looks from his dad.

Petey now lives in a small town with a loving lady, Carly, who feeds him, bathes him, and snuggles with him at bedtime. She thinks her little Chiweenie is perfect!

Petey has a longer body than his neighborhood Chihuahuas and he's taller, too. Only one ear stands up straight and his snout or nose is long and pointy. But being a Chiweenie, Petey has a special marking that gives his breed away – a pink spot on the tip of his black nose.

Because Petey is not a pure Chihuahua dog, he is made fun of and is constantly teased by the other dogs in the neighborhood, so Petey found other critters to play with – the bunnies!

Petey plays with the big and little bunnies all day long. They like that he runs fast, jumps high, and rolls in the grass. He even cuddles with them at naptime. The bunnies don't like the other dogs though; they bark at them and try to catch them. The other dogs are not like Petey – he just wants to have fun.

And, the fun they have! Sunshine or rain, they play every day until the humans start returning home from their jobs, then the bunnies go back to their underground homes and Petey returns to Carly.

One morning, when Petey arrives at the grassy knoll, he finds all the bunnies in a circle shaking and scared, talking about the close call one of the adult rabbits had with a coyote. They told Petey the coyote had been showing up very early in the morning to catch a bunny for himself.

Petey stood tall and shouted, "No coyote is a match for me. I'll protect you all!"

The other Chihuahuas were standing nearby and started laughing at Petey. Then Spanky, one of the meanest in the pack, spoke up, "You only like to play with bunnies! You're no match for a wild coyote!"

Petey looked around and saw the fear in his little bunny friends' eyes. He wasn't going to let them down.

"You just watch me! I'll protect my friends and get rid of that coyote for good!"

The other dogs just walked away together, waving Petey down and laughing.

The bunnies surrounded their big friend and hugged him and thanked him for wanting to help.

Squiggy, the oldest rabbit in the group spoke up, "We know you can do it, Petey. You can do anything you put your mind to!"

At the end of the day, Petey went home to Carly. He had to admit he was feeling scared about confronting the coyote in the morning while he sat quietly in a corner. Carly was worried about her little Chiweenie, so she scooped him up and danced and sang her favorite song to him. "You are my sunshine. My only sunshine. You make me happy when skies are grey..."

Carly's voice and gentle hug made Petey feel a whole lot better and he soon fell asleep in her arms.

Very early the next morning, Petey took a deep breath and headed for the knoll to chase away the coyote. As he walked from the safety of his home, he kept repeating to himself, "You can do this. Your friends are counting on you. You can chase the pesky coyote away! Just be like your mama!"

When he turned the corner, he could see the coyote on the hill. *Oh no! He has Squiggy!* Petey was no longer scared and ran as fast as he could toward the coyote.

"Put him down! Put my friend down!" Petey yelled as he ran straight at the coyote. But the coyote didn't budge.

"You don't frighten me, little dog," the coyote said to Petey when they were nose-to-nose.

"I won't let you hurt any of my friends, so let loose of Squiggy – now!" The hair on Petey's back was standing on end, and he looked fierce, as fierce as he could.

Then a familiar voice from behind Petey spoke loudly, "Put down the bunny and GO!" A large shadow grew behind and then over Petey until it met the coyote.

The coyote dropped Squiggy on the grass and backed up.

"Now leave and never come back here!" Petey boasted.

Petey began to chase the coyote off the knoll, down the street, and back out into the desert where he belongs. "Good riddance to you!" Petey hollered as he watched the coyote disappear.

When Petey returned to the grassy knoll, all the bunnies were hopping around and celebrating. Then it got quiet when Spanky started talking, "You did good, Petey. You kept your word and stood up to that coyote. I'm sorry that I made fun of your spotted nose, and I'd very much like to be your friend, too. If you'll have me."

Petey looks about and saw the other dogs making a circle around him. *Me too! Me too! And me!*

Petey looked up at Carly who had come to help fight off her little Chiweenie's foe, then smiled.

"Of course! We can all be friends; it'll be more fun that way!" Petey was very happy that all the dogs and bunnies would finally play happily together.

Watch for more adventures with Petey coming very soon to all the usual online stores!